MySELF  Bookshelf

Tortoise and Hare

By YeShil Kim

Illustrated by Rashin Kheiriyeh

Language Arts Consultant: Joy Cowley

NORWOOD HOUSE PRESS
Chicago, Illinois

DEAR CAREGIVER MySELF ▯▮▯ Bookshelf is a series of books that support children's social emotional learning. SEL has been proven to promote not only the development of self-awareness, responsibility, and positive relationships, but also academic achievement.

Current research reveals that the part of the brain that manages emotion is directly connected to the part of the brain that is used in cognitive tasks, such as: problem solving, logic, reasoning, and critical thinking—all of which are at the heart of learning.

SEL is also directly linked to what are referred to as 21st Century Skills: collaboration, communication, creativity, and critical thinking. MySELF Bookshelf offers an early start that will help children build the competencies for success in school and life.

In these delightful books, young children practice early reading skills while learning how to manage their own feelings and how to be considerate of other perspectives. Each book focuses on aspects of SEL that help children develop social competence that will benefit them in their relationships with others as well as in their school success. The charming characters in the stories model positive traits such as: responsibility, goal setting, determination, patience, and celebrating differences. At the end of each story, you will find a letter that highlights the positive traits and an activity or discussion to help your child apply SEL to his or her own life.

Above all, the most important part of the reading experience is to have fun and enjoy it!

Sincerely,

Shannon Cannon

Shannon Cannon, Ph.D.
Literacy and SEL Consultant

Norwood House Press • P.O. Box 316598 • Chicago, Illinois 60631
For more information about Norwood House Press please visit our website at www.norwoodhousepress.com or call 866-565-2900.

Shannon Cannon – Literacy and SEL Consultant
Joy Cowley – English Language Arts Consultant
Mary Lindeen – Consulting Editor

Library of Congress Cataloging-in-Publication Data
    Kim, YeShil.
    Tortoise and Hare / by YeShil Kim ; illustrated by Rashin Kheiriyeh.
        pages cm. -- (MySelf bookshelf)
    Summary: "After losing an embarrassing race against Tortoise, Hare challenges Tortoise to another race. While tricking Tortoise several times and cheating to get ahead, Hare ends up losing the race, for the second time. Realizing that losing isn't all that bad, Hare promises to be honest and fair if they race again"-- Provided by publisher.
    ISBN 978-1-59953-665-1 (library edition : alk. paper) -- ISBN 978-1-60357-725-0 (ebook)
    [1. Turtles--Fiction. 2. Hares--Fiction. 3. Racing--Fiction. 4. Winning and losing--Fiction. 5. Honesty--Fiction.] I. Kheiriyeh, Rashin, illustrator. II. Title.
    PZ7.K55997To 2015
    [E]--dc23
                                    2014030347

Manufactured in the United States of America in Stevens Point, Wisconsin.
263N—122014

Hare was dozing in the sun
when he saw Tortoise walk past.
At once, Hare was alert and angry.
The last time Hare had met Tortoise
was when that slowpoke
had beaten him in a race.
Hare was still embarrassed.

5

Hare called, "Tortoise! Hey, Tortoise!"
He hopped over and said,
Do you want to have another race?

Tortoise stared at him. "All right.
Will you have a nap like last time?"

That made Hare furious.
"This time I will beat you!"
he bellowed.

6

7

8

"Get set! Go!"

The second race began.
Hare hopped very fast.
Tortoise crawled and crawled.

When Hare looked back,
he saw Tortoise was far behind.
But Hare was not taking any chances.

9

Nearby, a monkey was eating a banana.
Hare grabbed the banana peel
and threw it in front of Tortoise.

When Tortoise stepped on the banana peel,
he slipped and flipped over onto his back.

Hare ran back into the race.

11

12

Hare was feeling hot.
When he saw the ice-cream cart,
he stopped and bought
a delicious ice-cream treat.
He was so busy eating
and talking to his friends
that he forgot about the race.
But what was this?
Tortoise was crawling past.

Hare could not believe it!
He ran and ran to pass Tortoise.

Hare thought he would
put Tortoise out of the race.
He got a shovel and dug a deep hole.
Then he covered the hole with sticks.
Tortoise would fall in the hole
and be stuck. Ha ha!

Sure enough,
Tortoise fell in the hole.
Hare laughed and laughed.
Tortoise couldn't get out of the hole.
Now Hare would win the race for sure.

Ouch!

16

17

Hare was not in a hurry
to get to the finish line.
He met up with his friends
and played some games.
But wait! A surprise!
Tortoise was crawling past.
That was impossible!
How did he get out of the hole?

19

Hare was very annoyed.
He put a sign on the road that said:
ROAD CLOSED. DETOUR.
The sign pointed to a path
that went far away
from the finish line.

ROAD CLOSED.
DETOUR.

Tortoise looked at the sign
and then went down the path.

Hare watched him go.
"I won't waste time," said Hare.
"Now I'll run to the finish line."

But something amazing happened.
As Hare ran toward the finish line,
slowpoke Tortoise crawled over it.
"No!" cried Hare. "No, no, no!"

22

23

This is what happened.
When Tortoise slipped
on the banana peel,
the monkey helped him.

Tortoise went on with the race.

24

The tortoise who passed
the ice-cream cart
and then fell in the hole
was one of Tortoise's brothers.

Tortoise went on with the race.

The tortoise who passed Hare
playing games with his friends
was the tortoise who went
down the wrong path.
He was Tortoise's other brother!

Meanwhile, Tortoise went on with the race.

Slowly but surely,
Tortoise won the race.

Hare kicked his feet and cried.

"How did you do it?

Tortoise, how did you win?"

"Hare, don't cry," said Tortoise.

"It's not important who wins or loses,

only that you do your best!

Everyone knows you are the fastest.

If you had played fair, you would have won."

Then Tortoise went to find his brothers.

Hare was so ashamed,

he could not lift his head.

The next time, he would play fair.

Dear Tortoise,

Everyone knows you are slow, but I was beaten by you two times! I was embarrassed and ashamed.

Now I need to thank you because you taught me a lesson. I have always been scared of losing, but I learned there is something more important than winning.

I need to be honest and fair and do the best I can. If you will agree to a third race with me, I promise to play fair.

Your friend, Hare

SOCIAL AND EMOTIONAL LEARNING FOCUS

Fair Play

There is a saying, "Cheaters never prosper." This is true for Hare. Instead of working hard and playing fair, his cheating ways cost him the race. There is another saying, "It's not whether you win or lose, it's how you play the game."

You can be a good sport and have fun whether you win or lose. Making "Fair Play Pennants" can help you show others what it means to be a good sport.

- You will need several pieces of 8 ½" x 11" paper, markers, a long piece of yarn or string, and possibly pictures from magazines. Be sure to get permission from an adult before cutting pictures.

- Cut the blank paper diagonally to create the pennant.

(continued on next page)

- Write a rule for fair play on each pennant.

- Draw pictures or cut and glue pictures from magazines on your pennants.

- After you have made several pennants, fold the edge over the string or yarn and staple them so you can hang them.

Here are a few ideas for the rules of good sportsmanship:

- Treat Others as You Would Like to Be Treated
- Encourage Your Teammates
- Avoid Arguments

- Win with Grace
- Cheer not Heckle
- Accept the Results

Reader's Theater

Reader's Theater is an interactive approach to reading that allows students to understand each story through dramatic interpretation. By involving students in reading, listening, and speaking activities, they provide an integrated approach for students to develop fluency and comprehension. A Reader's Theater edition of this book is available online. You can access the script by scanning the QR code to the right or visit our website at: http://www.norwoodhousepress.com/tortoiseandhare.aspx